Code & Silas Mysteries

Vilia Amertil

Published by Vilia Amertil, 2022.

This is a work of fiction. Similarities to real people, places, or events are entirely coincidental.

CODE & SILAS MYSTERIES

First edition. August 3, 2022.

Copyright © 2022 Vilia Amertil.

ISBN: 979-8223491668

Written by Vilia Amertil.

Also by Vilia Amertil

Code & Silas Mysteries
Code & Silas, You Again

Polly Parish Mysteries
Polly Parish Mysteries Book 2

The Night Cats
The Night Cats - The Arañar Rose

Standalone
Code & Silas Mysteries
Polly Parish Mysteries Book 1
The Night Cats
There Goes My Shorts
Murder Says Hi

Table of Contents

Code & Silas - Past Forgotten 1
Code & Silas - Garden Rust 16
Code & Silas - Run and Hit 32

Code & Silas - Past Forgotten

The first day back at Morrison Cox Elementary School and the chattering young students were bustling about as they greeted their friends. Christmas break was over and two weeks of not seeing each other face to face was disastrous for some and a relief for others.

All the teachers were back except for Mr. Turner, who had the flu and who was home sick. As usual after every Christmas break the principal, Mrs. Janice Turner, not related to the teacher home with the flu, would gather everyone in the auditorium to welcome them back. And as a sign that the holidays were officially over, she would give everyone a candy cane. Most of the canes never reached outside the auditorium because they were eaten by the students while listening, or attempting to listen, to the principal give her speech.

With all that over, classes began. And one of those classes was taught by Code Patterson, a fourth grade math teacher at the school. There were only two math teachers. The other being Mrs. Sarah Finch, who was the only other person not present for the principal's speech. Her car was in the parking lot but there was no sign of her.

"I see you're keeping tradition alive," Miss Patterson said, after Dexter tried to enter the classroom just as she was about to close the door. "And why are you late again?"

"I was–"

"Let me see, trying to stop aliens from invading the earth," she said, smiling.

"Miss Patterson, you read my mind," Dexter said, walking over and taking his seat at his desk.

"No, Dexter, I know you very well," she said. She was about to say something else when she heard her name being called over the intercom; she was being summoned to the principal's office.

"Miss Patterson is in t-r-o-u-b-l-e," Dexter teased.

"Not as much as you'll be if you keep coming to my class late and failing," she told him.

"Sorry," he said.

"Lindsey, you're in charge until I get back."

She had no idea why Principal Turner would want to see her. But it must be important enough for her to be called out during class, especially the first class of the day.

When she got to the office, the secretary told her that she could go right in. They're waiting for her. *They,* she whispered to herself.

"Ah, Miss Patterson," Principal Turner said, as she came in, "this is Detective Silas Armstrong."

"You have some information about my father's murder?" she asked.

"Excuse me," he said, looking puzzled.

"No, Miss Patterson, he's here concerning Mrs. Finch."

"Oh, I'm sorry. What about Mrs. Finch?"

"She's missing," he said.

"Her car is in the parking lot," she said.

"Her car is there. But she's nowhere on this school campus," Principal Turner said.

"What?" Code asked.

"Her husband said that she's missing," Detective Armstrong said.

"Missing?" Code asked.

"Let me make this conversation that seems to be going in circles more clearer," Detective Armstrong said.

"No need to be rude," Code told him.

"Sorry," he said, as if brushing some nusiance out of the way. "Mrs. Finch hasn't been seen since last night after 8 p.m. After church, she told her husband that she was going to stop off here at the school."

"That's why her car is here," Code said.

Detective Armstrong gave a slight frown, which she noticed, before speaking again. "He tried calling her but her phone was off. Police are checking her car as we speak."

"Do you think something bad happened to her?" Principal Turner asked.

"We don't know. It hasn't been twenty-four hours."

"You're kidding, right? Anything can–"

"Miss Patterson, twenty-four hours is–"

"A time when anything can happen," she said.

"When was the last time you saw or spoke with her?" he asked.

"Last day of school before Christmas break."

"Do you have any idea where she may be?"

"No."

"Thanks for your time," he said, turning away from her. "And thank you, Principal Turner. It would be a great help if you could also ask your staff if they know where she could be."

"I will. Anything I can do to help," she said.

"Thank you," he said, walking past Code as if she wasn't there.

"His father was the former principal of this school, you know," Principal Turner said, after he was gone.

"Well, he failed his father by not having any manners. I have to return to my class."

"Yes, yes. Go."

When she returned to her class, Lindsey was sitting at her table as the rest of the students were reading at their desks.

"You'll make a good teacher," she told her before reclaiming her chair at the table.

"Thanks, Miss Patterson."

"Now with the time we have left, who's ready for some math challenge?"

A chorus of yeses went up as Code looked out her classroom window just in time to see Mrs. Finch's car being towed.

"Challenge away," Dexter said, smiling.

Skipping her normal routine of staying behind after school, Code went to visit Mr. Finch instead. After letting her in, they went into the kitchen where they sat at the table as they drank coffee.

"Do you have any idea who would want to harm your wife?" she asked him.

"That's just it, no one would want to hurt her," he said. "You know, Laura, she was very nice."

"Is very nice," she corrected him.

"Yes, that's what I meant," he said, lifting his cup and taking a sip of his coffee. "But."

"But what?"

"In cases like this they always suspect the husband first," he said.

"You have nothing to worry about," she told him.

"That's what Detective Armstrong said before he added if you're innocent."

She politely smiled. She then asked, "Can you tell me about the last time you saw her? What was she wearing?"

"Okay. But I had told the detective already."

She listened as he told her what she needed to know. And while she was sitting in his kitchen, Detective Armstrong was at his desk in the police station. He was looking over the contents that were found in Mrs. Finch's car.

Nothing except one item interested him. A receipt for a bottle of milk. *If she bought that milk on the way to school that night, then that meant she wasn't planning on staying long,* he said to himself. He headed to the gas station only to find Code exiting the store as he was walking towards the door. He was going to ignore her after she walked by him. But instead he found himself calling out her name.

"Miss Patterson," he said, causing her to turn around.

"Code, please," she said.

"I think we got off on the wrong foot this morning, and for that I apologize," he said.

"Accepted," she said, as he was about to enter the store.

"The gas station video footage showed her buying the milk and then getting back into the car. No one followed her," she told him.

"They let you see the footage?" he asked in surprise.

"I told them that–"

"I don't care what you told them, this is a police investigation."

"Mrs. Finch is my friend."

"Listen, Miss Patterson."

"Code, please."

"Don't interfere with this investigation," he told her.

"I'm only trying to help," she said.

"Good day, Miss Patterson," he said, entering the gas station store only to come right back out with his phone to his ear.

Rushing over to his car, he jumped in and sped off, siren blaring like an urgent announcement warning people to watch out and not be in the way.

Arriving on the scene, he met other officers there. A park bench was cordoned off with police tape as a woman sat on it, as if frozen in time. Given the description of the clothes she was wearing, he immediately knew that it was Mrs. Finch.

"What do we have here?" he asked one of the officers on the scene.

"Female in her late forties."

"She's fifty."

"Oh. No sign of bruising."

"Who called it in?"

"Jogger," the officer said, pointing at a female jogger who looked to be in her twenties. "She said that she jogged past the victim forty-five minutes before coming back and meeting her in the same spot and position."

Detective Armstrong looked around before saying, "Don't look like any cameras nearby."

"No, sir."

"Thanks," he said, tapping the officer on the elbow before walking over to where the body was.

She looked so peaceful, as if she was sitting there quietly enjoying the serenity. Her eyes were closed and her hands were on her lap.

"Don't know what the cause of death is, not yet," said Mark Flores, forensic pathologist.

"I see no visible signs of injury," Detective Armstrong said.

"Nope."

"The last bench," he said.

"Huh?"

"Whoever brought her here walked past five other benches to place her on the last bench."

"They weren't in a hurry."

"Or this bench means something. After you remove the body turn the bench over, please."

"What?"

"Just humor me."

"As you wish."

His request was granted. And when the bench was turned over, there was something carved under it. You'll Always Be Remembered J.S.

"Check that out," Mark Flores said, "someone is taking pictures."

"Huh?" Turning around, Detective Armstrong saw Miss Patterson using her phone to take pictures. "Bored math teacher," he said.

"Oh."

"I'm going to inform the husband. Let me know what you find. Thanks," he said, before walking off.

"Will do."

When Mr. Finch found out that his wife was dead, he was inconsolable. He couldn't stop crying, no matter the comforting words the detective told him. He left him in that state, even though he asked if there was someone he could have called to come be with him. Mr. Finch told him that he wanted to be alone.

It was getting late. But before going back to the station, he decided to go back to where they found the body. He knew why. Because there was the reason he came back. Someone was under the bench using a flashlight to see.

"Anything interesting, Miss Patterson?" he asked.

"Code, please," she said, crawling from underneath the bench.

"We should have carried it," he said.

"I don't think you'll find much. But maybe–"

"But maybe and goodnight," he said, as he started to walk away.

"But maybe you would have found this," she said, lifting something up in the air.

"Tweezers."

"No, what's between it."

"Goodnight, Miss Patterson," he said, turning around and walking away, causing her to run after him and grab his arm.

"Wait." He sighed heavily before turning around. "This is between it." His eyes opened wide. "A piece of torn cloth or something."

"How did we miss that?" he asked.

"Sometimes you might need a little help, especially from a bored math teacher."

"How did you–"

"Mark Flores and I frequent the same diner."

"This town is way too small," he said.

"And yet you moved back here," she told him, handing him the tweezers.

"Shine the flashlight on it, please." After she did, he pulled an evidence bag out of his jacket pocket and placed the torn piece of whatever it could be into the bag. He then handed her back the tweezers.

"No, thanks, you can keep it," she said.

"I won't say goodnight again," he said, walking away with speed.

"You just did."

"It's not safe out here," he said, without looking back.

Taking his advice, she rushed over to her car. Not known to her, he waited and watched her leave before driving off. He headed directly to where Mark Flores was, the morgue.

"Appendicitis," Mark said.

"Huh?"

"That's what killed her, a busted appendix."

"So it wasn't murder?"

"Yes, it was."

"Flores."

"Sorry. There was bruising in that area, a lot of it. To me, it seemed as if the person repeatedly punched her there until her appendix burst."

"Interesting."

"Yeah."

"Take a look at this," he said, pulling the evidence bag out of his jacket pocket. "Oh, by the way loose lips."

"Oh, Code," he said, smiling.

"Is she actually named Code?" he asked.

"Yes. Her father gave her that name."

"About her father."

"Murder unsolved."

"I think there's a hair strand on this torn–"

"Piece of diner's apron where I eat. Where did you get this from?"

"Not me. But it was found under the bench where Mrs. Finch was found. The bench is no longer there. I told them to bring it in."

"I'll take a look at this."

"And the bench."

"Tomorrow. It's late. Wife and kid are waiting. You should try it some time."

"Wife and kids."

"No, a life."

"Hair."

Code drove to the gas station where Mrs. Finch had bought the milk and then to the park again. *It took twenty-five minutes to get here at normal speed,* she said to herself. *I doubt the person would have been speeding. And who is J.S.?*

Before heading home, she stopped over to see Mr. Finch, who now had family members over. She offered her condolences and any help if needed. Both were gladly received.

Finally home, she looked over the math workbooks of her students, got something to eat, took a shower and then took a quick peek at the photos she had taken. She was too sleepy to really focus on them. She headed to bed instead.

Bright and early, she made a quick stop at the diner. She got her usual and then headed to school. It finally sunk in when she pulled into the school's parking lot that Mrs. Finch was dead.

She felt tears streaming down her face. Resting her forehead on the steering wheel, she allowed them to fall on her lap. She jumped at a knock on her car window.

"Oh, I'm sorry. I didn't mean to startle you."

"Morning, Detective Armstrong."

"Are you okay?" he asked, noticing that she was crying.

"I'll be okay," she said, wiping the tears from her eyes. "Why are you here?" she asked as she exited her car.

"To pick up the teachers' statements about the last time they saw Mrs. Finch."

"She was murdered, wasn't she?"

"I think I'll be heading to the principal's office now," he said.

"Today isn't really a school day. They're bringing in grief counsellors. School will only be half day today."

"I guess it's for the best."

"In the photos I took yesterday there was a black van parked not too far from the park."

"You mean like the one parked across the street right now that probably followed you here," he said, with a calmness that surprised her. "Don't look," he said, before dashing off.

They had grief counselors come in to speak with the staff and students. It felt like deja vu for Code because a grief counselor also spoke with her after her father's death.

The children were sent home with their guardians; the teachers were also told that they could leave. Code left.

After Detective Armstrong had dashed off after the van, he never returned to see her. He did get the teachers' statements before heading to the diner. And when he walked in and noticed her, he knew he should have informed her of what had happened.

"It got away. Sorry," he told her. "But if that van is following you, you could be in danger."

"I was looking over some old photos of Mrs. Finch at our school's different functions over the years," she said.

"Miss Patterson, didn't you hear me?" he asked.

"I promise to be careful," she said, as he raised an eyebrow. "Extra careful. Anyway, I noticed this. Please sit."

He reluctantly took a seat at her table. "What is it?" he asked, noticing the diner aprons.

"This photo," she said, turning her laptop so he could take a look at the photo. "Look at the button on her husband's shirt."

"To J.S., Sadly Missed."

"I did some research. Jonathan Smith was found dead twenty-five years ago with a ruptured appendix. But he also had some bruising in that area. It's a cold case."

"Twenty-five minutes to get to the gas station to the park. How did the person know if she was stopping off at the gas station?"

"Even her husband didn't know."

"We need to talk with him," he said, getting up.

"We?"

"I mean I need to talk with him," he stressed, before leaving.

He did go alone, even though she was tempted to get into her car and drive over to Mr. Finch's house. She stayed seated as she looked over some more photos on her laptop.

Another photo captured her attention. Yes, Mr. Finch was in it as he wore the same button. But so was another person who also wore the same button.

She did some more research on Jonathan Smith, who had been staying at the orphanage. He was ten years old when he was found dead in the bushes at the back of the orphanage. Twenty-five-year-old volunteer Joshua Finch, along with an unnamed person, were the ones who found the body. *Unnamed person. Is this person in that photo the unnamed person?* she asked herself. She heard the chime of the door to the diner, and that person walked in, causing her to slowly close her laptop.

"Hi, Mark," she said.

"Oh. Hi, Code, have you seen Detective Armstrong?" he asked.

That mentioned detective was sitting in the living room of Mr. Finch as he was being given the full details of what had happened twenty-five years ago.

"It was horrible," Mr. Finch said. "I mean a person can never forget something like that. We all suspected that he had been beaten. And so did his older sister."

"And you thought someone at the orphanage did it, one of the workers?"

"I don't know, maybe. We were just volunteers on the weekends. Mark and I were–"

"Mark Flores?" asked Detective Armstrong.

"Yes. That was where I met my wife. She was a young teacher then."

"Let me get this straight, you, Mrs. Finch and Mark were all there when that incident happened."

"My wife took it pretty hard then. But over the years, she seemed to have forgotten all about it. She even became annoyed when I had mentioned it sometimes."

The detective was just about to ask something when the doorbell rang. Mr. Finch went to answer it. He returned with Mr. Flores.

"Code said that I'll find you here," Mark said. "A minute," he said, motioning with his head towards the door.

"Excuse me, Mr. Finch, I'll be right back," he told him, getting up and leaving. "What is it?" he asked Mark once they were outside. They walked towards Mr. Flores' car.

"That hair on that piece of apron belongs to Jonathan Smith."

"What?"

"I know. I ran it through the database. It's his."

"I know you were there when his death took place."

"Yeah, I was."

"Could Mrs. Finch have killed him?" Detective Armstrong asked as silently as he could.

"Over the years I came to that conclusion."

"Where is Miss Patterson?" he asked.

"When I left, she was talking with one of the waitresses at the diner."

"Was it the jogger?"

"What jogger?"

"The one who found the body."

"I think so."

"Code's in danger," he said, rushing to his car.

He went over to the diner; there was no sign of her or the waitress. The black van was parked in the back. He called to have it towed. Getting the address of where the waitress lived, he rushed over. When he got, there no one was there.

There were photos on the wall and he slowly scanned all of them. Nothing interesting until he got to the photo in her bedroom, which caused him to rush out of the house.

"I know it was you who carved that under the bench," Code said to the waitress who was walking behind her. "Can you untie me, please? This knot is too tight."

"Looks like I should have taped your mouth," she said.

"Then how were we going to have a lovely conversation."

"Stop talking."

"You know twenty-five plus twenty-five equals fifty, the age of Mrs. Finch. Twenty-five years ago, she killed your uncle. You're twenty-five."

"Stop it with the twenty-fives," she said, taking her to the place where her uncle's body had been found.

"Exactly why did we come back to the site of this old orphanage?" Code asked.

"I don't know," she said.

"Of course, since you weren't the one who killed her."

"Be quiet!" she screamed.

"So when did he find out that his wife had killed J.S.?"

"Last year. Married for all that time and had no idea that his wife was a murderer."

"And you're an accessory," Detective Armstrong said, coming into view with his gun drawn.

"I'll talk," she said, as she quickly put her hands up in the air.

"Please do," Code said.

"Wait until we get to the station," Detective Armstrong said.

"No, let me do it here. Mr. Finch told me where his wife was that night."

"How do you know Mr. Finch?" Code asked, causing the detective to clear his throat.

"He came into the diner one day; he said that I looked familiar. I told him who I was and it went from there. He told me about my uncle."

"What happened after you found out where she was?" Code asked.

"I followed her to the gas station after church. I called Mr. Finch and told him."

"And he told you to try to get her in your van," Detective Armstrong said.

"Yes, but I honestly didn't know what he was planning. After the gas station, there aren't any cameras or many lights."

"And was that where you stopped her car and put her into your van?" Code asked.

"Yes. Forcibly. He showed up and that's when we went to the park. I parked where we couldn't be seen. It didn't matter because no one else was around."

"And what happened next?" Code asked.

"Next," began Detective Armstrong, "is we finish this at the station." Another police car was on the scene. He waived the officer over; the waitress was taken into custody.

"You need to arrest Mr. Finch," she told the detective when they were alone. He smiled. "You've already arrested Mr. Finch," she said.

"Thanks to a photo of him and the waitress wearing that button," he said, as he was about to get into his car.

"Do you know what else happened?" she asked, hoping he would tell her.

"He went into the back of the van and locked the door. He and his wife argued about that incident. In his anger, he called her a murderer and did to her what she had done to Jonathan all those years ago."

"And then he carried her to that bench."

"Where the waitress had carved that message under it. She didn't know at that time that her apron was torn or that a strand of her uncle's hair was on it."

"But Mrs. Finch's car at the school."

"He drove it there and parked it where no school cameras could see. The waitress drove him back to the park. After that, they went their separate ways."

"She jogged that way like she did every morning and then called you guys about the body."

"Her conscience was her guide," Detective Armstrong said.

"I wish my father's murderer had one. Forget it."

"I'm heading to the station," he said, opening the door to his car. "Was that being extra careful?" he asked.

"I'm sorry, but I–"

"You're attracted to danger," he said.

"Not what I was going to say," she said.

"Goodbye, Miss Patterson."

"Code, please," she said, smiling.

He waited for her to get into her car before he got into his. When she drove off, he took out his phone and made a call.

"Get me everything you have about the Richard Patterson murder, please," he told the person on the other end.

Code & Silas - Garden Rust

As Code Patterson and her best friend, Maddie, were entering the art gallery to see the exhibition, Principal Janice Turner was exiting the gallery.

"Goodnight ladies," she said to them.

"Goodnight," they both said in unison.

"Principal Turner, I didn't know you liked art," Code said.

"Yes, art lover here," she said, smiling. "You ladies will enjoy it. Thirty-year-old Sasha Thomas is a great artist."

"Looks like she got your stamp of approval," Maddie said.

"Yes. I'm off. A bowl of chocolate ice cream and a good movie await me on this Friday night," she said, waving goodbye to them as she headed towards her car.

"It's so good to be up and about again," Maddie said, linking her arms with Code.

"It's nice to have you up and about," she told her as they entered the gallery.

Even though it wasn't packed, there were still a lot of people that came to see Ms. Thomas' work. She was a local artist who finally made it big; she came back to town to hold her first art exhibition.

The two teachers mixed into the crowd as they went from painting to painting.

"So, what do you think?" Maddie asked.

"Colorful," Code said.

"The one with the dancing daisies is my favorite," Maddie said.

"I wonder what's under that," Code said, heading towards a painting that was covered.

"That's for tomorrow night," a woman behind her said. Turning around, she saw Ms. Thomas standing there.

"Is your hand okay?" Maddie asked, noticing a bandage on her hand.

"I cut myself. I'll survive. That painting is about something I can't get out of my head."

"Exciting," Code said.

"I don't see it that way. Excuse me," she said, walking off.

"Did you say something to upset her?" Maddie asked.

"No. Did you notice that all her paintings have flowers in them? I wonder if this one does too," she said, turning to face the covered painting.

"Code," she said, tapping her friend's hand, "now I think she and the art gallery owner are arguing."

"Where?" she asked, turning to see. "That's Michael Mitchell."

"Should we stop for pizza afterwards?" she asked as they returned to the exhibition.

"Okay."

The next day that painting was removed, not to be seen by the public. The reason for it was on the front page of the newspaper that was waiting just outside Code's door the next morning. Local Artist, Sasha Thomas, Found Dead was the headline story. Not much information was given. Pulling her robe tighter around her, she went back inside.

Detective Armstrong, who was on the scene last night, was now on the scene again. What couldn't be seen because of the dark was seen with the light of day. *But why was she gardening in the dark?* he asked himself as he stood in the exact same spot where the body was found.

Some officers went through the house last night; he was going through it again. He was upstairs when he heard someone moving downstairs. Pulling out his weapon, he quietly went down. Seeing who it was, he put his weapon away.

"Miss Patterson, I didn't know you knew the victim," he said.

"Oh yes, I knew–"

"Knowing Sasha Thomas and knowing about Sasha Thomas are two different things."

"They said that she was found in her garden."

"Then what are you doing in here?"

"Because I have already been to the garden," she said, trying to make her way upstairs.

"And where are you going?"

"Not upstairs."

"Correct. You can go now."

"I guess I should give you these," she said, taking a napkin out of her purse.

"A napkin," he said.

"The things that are in the napkin," she told him, giving it to him.

Taking it, he slowly opened it. "Rusted nails. Thank you. Goodbye."

"I didn't touch them. I wore gloves."

"Good day, Miss Patterson."

"Code, please," she said, heading towards the door. "Before I go."

"Oh no."

"Any chance of me seeing that painting that was covered and was going to be put on display today?"

"Nope."

"Michael Mitchell, the gallery owner, said–"

"Of course, you went to the art gallery."

"He and Ms. Thomas were arguing last night."

"Goodbye," he said.

"Goodbye," she said, turning to leave.

Going to the door, he stood there and watched her leave before going back upstairs. He took a few things out of the house and went to see Mark Flores, the forensic pathologist.

"Down here," Mark said, noticing that the detective was trying to figure out where he was.

"What are you doing on the floor?" he asked.

"Trying to find this," he said, holding up a sewing needle.

"Was she killed with that?" Detective Armstrong asked.

"No, I am trying to sew my daughter's birthday present."

"Ms. Thomas."

"Tetanus."

"Tetanus?"

"Yes, to be exact, the bacterium Clostridium Tetani that causes tetanus. She had a cut on her hand. Did you guys find anything rusty in the garden?" The detective began smiling. "What's so funny?"

"Nothing. These were found in the garden," he said, taking out the napkin containing the nails.

"I'll test them to see if her DNA is on them."

"Who gardens that late? Or should I say very early in the morning? Even if she had lights, there was no way she could have seen those nails."

"Maybe someone put them there."

"Correct. What are you doing?" Detective Armstrong asked.

"Trying to thread this needle," he said, trying his best to put the thread through the eye of the needle he was holding up in the air.

"Anyway, I'm going to look at some art," he said, shaking his head at his friend before leaving.

Code's plan was to go back to the art gallery to see if she could get any information about that painting. She also wanted to know what that argument was about. But when she got there, the gallery was closed. Stumped as to where to go next, she went over to Maddie's house.

"I thought Girls Night In didn't start until seven tonight," Maddie said, letting her in.

"I know," she said, crossing her fingers and then uncrossing them, a habit she had since she was ten years old when she really wanted to do something but didn't know how to do it.

"What's the matter?"

"Huh?"

"Your fingers."

"Detective Armstrong has that painting," she said.

"What painting?" Maddie asked. "Never mind, the one from last night. You think that has a clue?"

"I don't know. But Ms. Thomas didn't seem too happy about it."

"Yeah, last night. I remember. Then why have it go on display?"

"Well it's not anymore. Enough about that. How's my best friend free of cancer doing?" she asked, giving her a hug.

"Great. I feel fine."

"Wonderful."

"I was just about to make a salad. Want one?"

"Sure," she said, crossing her fingers again.

"Do you want rocks in it?"

"Sure. Thanks."

"You aren't listening," Maddie said.

"Huh? Maddie."

"Yeah."

"How would you like to go to the police station?"

Detective Armstrong had been staring at the painting for eleven minutes and couldn't find one single clue that connected it to Ms. Thomas' murder. He got up and was about to walk away from it, but that was when he saw Miss Patterson being directed by another officer to his desk. Rushing back to try to cover the painting with the sheet, he failed when it slipped out of his hands and onto the ground.

"And now she has invaded my space," he joked.

"I'm here to help," she said.

"No, I think we here at the police station got it covered."

"What's the title of the painting?" she asked.

"Why are you here?" he asked.

"To find out the title of the painting," she said.

"Hope you enjoy your Saturday night."

"Oops, pardon me," said the cleaning lady, who was mopping.

"You're early tonight," he said, before returning his attention back to Miss Patterson.

She was about to say something but quickly turned away and began walking. "Goodnight," she said.

Scratching the back of his head, he said, "Miss Patterson."

"Code, please," she said quietly, as she slowly turned around.

"Did you and the cleaning lady get what you ladies came for?"

"I can't go to jail," Maddie said. "I have third grade English lesson to–"

"He's not going to arrest us." He didn't answer. "Are you going to arrest us?"

"Why are you so interested in this painting?" he asked.

"Because at the art gallery last night, she didn't seem to be happy about putting it on display. Excited, I should say."

"And you want to know why she was going to do it."

"Yes."

"The painting is a sad sunflower. Title of painting," he said, turning his back to her. He didn't know she had walked over to stand next to him.

"Sunflower Melancholy," she said.

"Okay, you–"

"That's wrong."

"What's wrong?" he asked.

"7 x 9 isn't 64," she said.

"What are you talking about?" both he and Maddie asked at the same time.

"Look around the edges, the borders of the painting she has 7 x 9 = 64. It's supposed to be 7 x 9 = 63."

She looked over at the detective to see if he knew if that meant anything. But he was good at hiding what exactly he was thinking when he had to.

"Nice to finally meet you," Maddie said, as she gently began pulling her friend away. "Goodnight."

"Goodnight."

"Why are we leaving?" Code asked.

"Because he isn't smiling," Maddie said.

"He seems to use that face a lot around me," she said, as they were standing outside the station.

Once they were gone, he sat down at his desk and typed something into his computer. He knew what 64 meant.

Everything about that incident was put out of their minds for that night, and Girls Night In was an enjoyable one. Code left at eleven o'clock to go home. Getting into her car, she started to pull away from Maddie's house. And that was when she noticed the house number. She turned off the engine.

Using her phone, she typed in something into the search box. Starting her car again, she drove off and to the place where house #64 used to be. It was burnt to the ground the night before Ms. Thomas' art show.

She was going to park her car in front of where the house used to be. But another car was already there.

Detective Armstrong was looking in his rearview mirror as he watched her get out of her car and walk towards his. She tapped on his window, and he rolled it down.

"Don't you ever sleep?" he asked.

"They're connected, aren't they?"

"What? Never mind. Don't you have lessons to plan."

"Did some of it at Girls Night In."

"What? Never mind."

"May I come in?"

"If I say no, will you leave?"

"Yes."

"Then you can't come in."

And to his surprise, she left. But that bothered him throughout the night because it was too easy. He was nowhere in sight when she came back at 6:15 a.m. She was dressed in all black with a pair of hiking boots on her feet. *I wonder who lived here?* she asked herself.

It was too early to knock on the neighbor's door to go ask that and some other questions. She brought up the article again about the house fire. It was abandoned. Not knowing what to do next, she headed home to do math lesson plans for her fourth grade class.

Meanwhile, Detective Armstrong was waiting for Mark Flores to show up at work. And when he did, the forensic pathologist gave him a puzzled look.

"Don't worry, I didn't sleep here in my car," the detective said.

"My sister is in town, I can–"

"Not set me up on a blind date, or any date."

"I worry about you," he said, looking for the key to his door.

"My dad says the same thing."

"You know, you and Code are similar."

"Miss Patterson and I are nothing alike. And what are you smiling at?"

"Nothing."

"Any related connections to the bones found under the floorboards of house #64 and Ms. Thomas?" he asked.

"Brother and sister. The brother had been missing for seven years before his bones were discovered. He was seventeen years old."

"Seven years is how long she's been away from this town. I'm sure her brother didn't crawl where his bones were discovered."

"Fractured skull."

"Cause of death?"

"Yes."

"She knew who the murderer was."

"And the murderer knew that she knew."

"Garden Rust," Detective Armstrong said.

"What?"

"I have to go," he said, rushing out.

He headed back to the station and looked up the missing case file. Everyone thought Adam Thomas had ran off after an argument with his father. Even though members of the family were suspected in his disappearance, they all had ironclad alibis.

Mr. Thomas had left on a fishing trip right after the argument. He was seen by at least twenty plus people. Mrs. Thomas had stayed at her sister's house to help during the time when her brother-in-law had died. Ms. Sasha Thomas was at an art show. All of them were ruled out. *Next door neighbor,* he said to himself. *I wonder if it's the same person who reported the fire.*

A lovely Sunday afternoon. Birds singing. Some people dressed up in their Sunday's best after coming from church. Some sitting on the porch. Some kids riding their bikes. And the car of a school teacher was parked in the driveway of the house that was standing next to a burnt structure.

"Detective Silas Armstrong?" an elderly woman asked.

"Yes, ma'am," he said.

"Code said that you'd be coming," she said, holding open the screen door. "Do come in."

On entering, he saw Miss Patterson sitting on the sofa. She was holding a plate full of cookies.

"Good day, Miss Patterson," he said, scratching the side of his neck.

"Good day, Detective Armstrong. Do you want a cookie?" There was no smile on his face. "I guess not," she said, resting the plate full of cookies on the coffee table.

"I'm Mrs. Eudora Phillips. I've lived here for forty-three years. And Ms. Sasha Thomas burnt down the house she grew up in."

Neither Detective Armstrong nor Code Patterson was expecting that announcement. He was standing when she made it but sat down immediately afterwards.

"Are you sure?" he asked the old lady.

"I might be seventy-four years old but I'm still in my right mind, so is my husband."

"Where is your husband?" he asked.

"Went fishing with Mr. Thomas."

"The same Mr. Thomas who used to live next door?" Code asked, causing the detective to clear his throat.

"Yes, they still go fishing together all the time."

"So none of them know about the fire," the detective said. "If Mr. Thomas doesn't know about the fire, then he doesn't know about his son's body being found or his daughter being murdered."

"Do you know how we can reach them?" Code asked.

"When they go up to Fish Man's Lodge it's no noise from the world. No phones. No radio. No TV."

"Fish Man's Lodge. I'm sending someone to go get them," he said, pulling out his phone and making a call for an officer to go and get them. After that was done he asked, "Are you sure she burnt down that house?"

"Yes, it's on camera. I told her that and she said that it was good. She said that the truth would finally come out."

"Do you know what she meant by that?" he asked.

"No, but she gave me this," she said, getting up and walking over to a table. She returned with a painting, a copy of Sunflower Melancholy.

"Mrs. Phillips," Code said.

"Eudora, please."

"Eudora," Code said, shooting a quick glance at Detective Armstrong.

"Miss Patterson," he stressed.

"Eudora, did they have sunflowers in their yard?" Code asked.

"They had no flowers in their yard."

"Was there anyone nearby that had sunflowers in their yard?" the detective asked.

"The Turners and–"

"Principal Janice Turner," Code said.

"Yes. Their yard was covered with it. Well, that's how they met it. The previous owner–"

"You mean they didn't plant those flowers," she said.

"Oh no, the Turners didn't plant them. They have only been living there for five years."

"Do you know who lived there before?" he asked.

"That I don't remember. They normally kept to themselves. But Sasha was close to the son."

They stayed with Mrs. Phillips for a little while before they both left. Code went to see Mrs. Turner; Detective Armstrong went to the police station to await the arrival of Mr. Thomas and Mr. Phillips.

It wasn't a long drive for Code; she arrived at the principal's house in no time. Mrs. Turner and her husband were sitting on the porch when they saw her walking up the steps.

"Miss Patterson, what a surprise," said Mrs. Turner. "Is anything the matter?"

"No, I was visiting Mrs. Phillips and she told me that you lived nearby. Lovely house."

"Yes. Quiet neighborhood."

"Except for the fire the other night," Mr. Turner said.

"This might seem like an odd question, but do you know who was the previous owner of your house?"

"The Mitchells," Mr. Turner said.

"Michael Mitchell, the art gallery owner, used to live here?" she asked.

"And one of the firefighters that came the other night," Mrs. Turner said. "Why do you asked?"

"Oh, no reason. I have to go," she said, rushing to her car.

Mr. Thomas was in a state of shock when he received the news about his only two children. He was grateful that his good friend, Mr. Phillips, was there. Detective Armstrong, sensitive to the situation, was gentle with the questions. He gained some information, including some about the Mitchells.

And when they both left, that was where his mind stayed, on the Mitchells. He couldn't bring Michael and Matthew in for questioning.

There was no proof that they did anything wrong, not seven years ago and not recently. But the sunflowers. That he couldn't get out of his mind either.

"Michael was the art gallery owner. He was closer to Sasha than his brother. I guess that's why they got along," he said to Mark after he had made his way down there to see him.

"Yeah, but what does he have to do with Adam Thomas?"

"And then there's that argument that he had with Sasha. I'm going to talk with him and his brother," he said, heading towards the door.

"Wait, what do you think?" he asked, holding up what looked like a blouse.

"Is it a blouse?" he asked.

"Of course. Believe me, it's a blouse. It's my twelve-year-old daughter's birthday gift."

"I'm sure she'll love it," he said, walking away.

"That doesn't sound convincing," he said, holding it up again. He smiled to himself.

Both Code and Maddie were done with their lesson plans and had a free Sunday night. After Code suggested it to her friend, they headed to the art gallery. It was opened again with Ms. Thomas' work still on display. More people were in there than on Friday night. Sunflower Melancholy wasn't on display. It was still at the police station.

They had seen all the paintings, but that wasn't the reason Code went back there. She wanted to talk with Michael, who was nowhere in sight. He suddenly appeared after ten minutes, and he looked upset. His brother, Matthew, was standing right behind him, and he also looked upset.

"They looked like they'd been arguing," Maddie said.

"If only I knew about what," Code said, heading in their direction, even though Maddie was trying to stop her.

"Great turnout," she said, as she approached them.

"Yes, it is Miss Patterson," Michael said. "I don't think you've met my brother. This is Matthew."

"Hello, Miss Patterson," Matthew said.

"Hello, Matthew. Do you like art too?" she asked.

"No, not really. Please excuse me. It was nice meeting you," he said, walking off but returning with the detective on the case. "Michael, Detective Armstrong would like to ask us some questions."

"Okay, we can go into my office."

"Goodnight, Miss Patterson," the detective said to her. "You can stop trying to hide your face with that book. I knew it was you the moment I started to walk over this way," he whispered to her before walking off with the two brothers.

After seven minutes later, only the detective exited the office. "And?" she asked.

"And I'm surprised you didn't stand by the office door and try to listen in," he said.

"She did," Maddie said.

"Gosh Maddie, thanks. I couldn't hear anything anyway."

"It's school tomorrow," he said, walking off and out of the gallery.

After Code dropped Maddie home, she also went home. She remembered the photo of the painting that she had secretly taken when she was in the police station. Taking her phone out of her purse, she turned it on and found the photo. She slowly scanned it and, for the first time, noticed something.

Detective Silas Armstrong noticed that same thing too as he sat in the police station looking at the painting. Grabbing his coat, he rushed to his car. *I have to go back to that gallery,* he said to himself.

But Code beat him there. The gallery was almost empty as she headed to Michael's office. Only Matthew was there.

"Miss Patterson," he said, "are you looking for Michael? He stepped out but will be back shortly."

"No, I'm looking for you," she said, causing him to get up from out of the chair he was sitting in.

"Why?"

"Seven years ago why."

"That was an accident," he said, moving closer to the door and trying to close it, only to have it pushed open by Detective Armstrong.

"A fractured skull accident," the detective said.

"We were playing and I pushed him. I panicked and called my dad."

"And he helped you to bury that body," he said.

"Yes, I'm sorry."

"Ms. Thomas' death wasn't an accident," Code told him.

"I always felt she knew what we had done, but just couldn't prove it. And then Michael showed me that painting and I knew for sure she knew."

"The border," Detective Armstrong said. "Just one small part of the border had 7 + 9, which is 16, the age you were when that incident happened. And 64 was reversed to 46, the age of your father back then."

"Michael had told me that Sasha had cut her hand during the process of setting up for her art show. Stubborn as she was, she kept on going and wasn't too concern about the cut on her hand."

"How long ago was that?" Code asked.

"About two weeks before her show. The night her cut happened, I went over to her house with some rusty nails I had lying around my house. I wanted to talk with her, change her mind."

"But she wouldn't change it," Detective Armstrong said.

"No. So before I left, I walked over to her garden and put them in it. I made sure she saw me near the garden. I knew she wouldn't have time to do a proper check of what it was that I put in it."

"Because she was very busy with putting her show together," Detective Armstrong said.

"Yes," Matthew said.

"But you knew that she would have gone to look in her garden again, maybe on a different night," Code said.

"Yes. That night I was there, I watched her walk over and bend down. I heard when she said, 'Ow.' And I knew the nails had done their job. And all I had to do was wait until–"

"The arrival of tetanus," Code said.

"And Michael filled me in, innocently, about her health status and her unwillingness to see a doctor. That's why they argued."

"Did you know she was the one who burnt down their house?" Detective Armstrong asked.

"Yes. She was pushing for the truth to come out."

"But you couldn't have that," Code said.

"Matthew Mitchell, I'm arresting you for the murder of Sasha Thomas and for causing the death of her brother Adam Thomas seven years ago."

He was read his rights and was being led out in handcuffs when his brother returned. Michael was shocked to see and hear what was happening. He had no idea.

"Ready for another school week?" Detective Armstrong asked as he and Code were standing outside the gallery.

"Always ready," she said. "She was pushing for the truth to come out. What am I pushing for with my father's death? Forget it. I'll buy you a cup of coffee," she said, smiling.

"Sorry, but I have somewhere to be," he told her.

"Hot date," she said jokingly.

"No."

"Goodnight, Silas," she said.

"Goodnight, Miss Patterson."

"Maybe one day you'll call me Code," she said, walking away.

The place he had to be was the same place Mark had to be, the spot where they had found Richard Patterson's body ten years ago.

"One thing Code has been teaching me without her knowing is looking at photos more intently," Detective Armstrong said.

"Does she know you call her Code?" Mark asked.

"No, and she will not find out," he said.

"These lips are sealed."

"What's that next to his feet in the corner? It's barely noticeable," Detective Armstrong said, handing a photo of the crime scene to Mark, who held it up.

"It looks like a tag, a name tag. Top letters ORP," he said.

"CORP."

"Bottom letters LER."

"Miller. Terrence Miller of Sandbook Corporation. We have a suspect."

Code & Silas - Run and Hit

It was two o'clock in the morning and Code Patterson couldn't sleep. She was trying to remember something that had happened ten years ago. But every time she got to what it could be, it seemed as if something was blocking it. Getting up out of bed, she walked over to a desk in her room. Pulling out her bag, she took out the marked math quiz test papers and looked over them again. *Dexter is a very smart kid,* she said to herself. *He's the only one that got 100%.* She left the papers and headed into the kitchen.

Turning on the light, she walked over to the fridge and opened it. There wasn't anything special that she wanted, so she closed the door. She was restless. She was about to turn off the light and walk out of the room when she noticed a handprint on the window above the sink. It was on the outside. Curiosity was like a nice warm coat on a cold day. And engulfed in it, she went out. She wasn't expecting what she found.

Seven minutes later, police cars were all over her neighborhood. One of those cars had Detective Silas Armstrong.

"Well, Miss Patterson," he said, "looks like this suspicious death came directly to your doorstep."

"So you think it's murder," she said, hoping he would tell her more.

"Do you know the victim?" he asked.

"No," she answered.

"Did you touch anything?"

"No."

"Do you–"

"Need my help."

"I wasn't going to ask that. I guess that'll be it for tonight," he said, walking away and approaching an officer in uniform.

She watched him and tried to figure out what he was saying. He noticed and smiled at her. She nervously smiled back.

The body was taken away as the police wrapped up their presence on the scene. They all left, including Detective Armstrong, or so she thought. She went over to where the body was found and, even though it was dark, bent down and started looking around.

"How long have you been standing there?" she asked, feeling a presence behind her.

"Long enough to tell you that some light would be better to see," Detective Armstrong said.

"I would have used a flashlight but that would have brought attention. Don't want the neighbors to see me," she said, standing to her feet.

"Like the neighbor standing and looking at you from across the street."

Quickly turning in that direction, she saw who it was. "Goodnight, Ms. Harris."

"Are you okay?" Ms. Harris asked.

"Yes, he's a detective," she said, pointing at Detective Armstrong.

"You're not in trouble, are you?"

"You do know it's very early in the morning, right?" Detective Armstrong said to her.

"Sorry. I'm okay. Goodnight, Ms. Harris," she said.

"Goodnight, Code," Ms. Harris said, going back into her house.

"Goodnight, Miss Patterson," he said, not moving.

"Oh, you're waiting for me to go in." He smiled. "Oh my goodness, that's the second time you smiled. Are you okay?" There wasn't any more smile on his face. "I'm going. Goodnight, Silas."

He watched her go inside before he left. There wasn't much investigation he could do so he headed home. He didn't go to bed but sat on his living room sofa. Taking out a crime scene photo out of the Richard Patterson file, he held it up. *A blind man and a fingerprint with no owner,* he said to himself. Leaning back on the sofa, he fell asleep only to wake up in another hour by the sound of his phone ringing.

"Detective Armstrong, this is Sgt. Jones, I've got a woman here at the station claiming that the body found early this morning is her son."

"How did she know a body was found?" he asked through a yawn.

"Social media."

"I'll be right there," he said, yawning again.

There was no way Code could get back to sleep, even though she needed some. School was going to start in a few hours. And she had been up since two o'clock in the morning. There was no point in going back outside to see if there was something she could find where the body was found. So, there she sat at her kitchen table, drumming her fingers on it.

Then she remembered the jacket the victim was wearing had a crest or something on it. *If it is local, then it should be easy to find,* she thought.

And so it was, Warrenstone College. Going to the college's website, she went through almost everything that was on it. She was about to close the pages when she noticed a photo of the person that was in her yard. Unknown to her, it was the same person that the woman in the police station was telling Detective Armstrong about.

"Yes, the same person you just described is the person we found tonight," Detective Armstrong said.

"My name is Mrs. Maria Warren," she said. "That young man is my twenty-year-old son, Jasper Warren."

"We're very early in our investigation, but can you make an official identification later today?" he asked.

"Yes," she said, trying to hold back her tears.

He was about to offer her a napkin when someone else did. "I'm sure the police will do their best to solve this crime," Code said.

The detective rubbed the back of his neck, as if there was a pain in it. "Mrs. Warren, I'll send a police car over to your house," he told her as he gently helped her to her feet.

After another officer got her details, they both watched her leave. And after she was gone, Detective Armstrong slowly turned and looked at Code.

"Before you say anything, let me–"

"Leave the station."

"I'll have to call a taxi again," she said.

"Why?" he asked.

"I'm too sleepy to drive," she said.

"Then that's why you should have stayed home."

"His name is Jasper Warren, but I think you already know that. He's a junior at–"

"What time does school start?" he asked.

"I have to be there in forty-five minutes."

"That explains why you're dressed up looking like that's where you're supposed to be. Was that a yawn?"

"Code," a voice behind her said.

"Maddie," she said, turning around.

"Is she here to take you to school?" he asked.

"Yes, she is."

"Goodbye, Miss Patterson."

"Code, please," she said, through a very big yawn.

Watching her leave, he gently shook his head and smiled. He looked at his watch and also left the station. All dressed up in his coat suit after a quick shower, he headed to Warrenstone College.

News of the death had already spread through the campus. That was where he found the best friend of the deceased.

"And that was the last time you saw him, around 9:33 p.m."

"Yes."

"And you are?"

"James Miller."

That surname caused Detective Armstrong to raise an eyebrow. "Any relation to a Terrence Miller?"

"He was my dad."

"Was?"

"He was killed ten years ago in a hit and run that has never been solved."

"I'm sorry."

"Thanks."

"Do you have any idea where Mr. Warren was going after you left him?"

"Nah."

"Okay, thanks," he said, walking off and heading to the dean's office.

As he was sitting in the dean's office, Miss Patterson was standing before a class of fifteen vibrant students. She was feeding off their energy, even though she was still sleepy.

"I marked your test papers last night and . . ."

"And!" they all screamed, knowing the routine of her keeping them in suspense every time she marked test papers.

"And I'm happy to say that everyone did very well."

"Yay!" they all screamed.

"Are we going to get a star and a smiley face?" Dexter asked.

"Of course," she said, wearing a big smile on her face.

"Math is important," the whole class said.

"You guys have been paying attention," she told them.

"Except for this person," said Dexter.

"Who?"

"I found this piece of paper on my way to school this morning," he said.

"What paper?"

"I don't know whose paper it is. I just picked it up."

"Dexter."

"Sorry, I'll throw it in the garbage," he said, getting up to go do that.

"It's okay. Please give it to me and I'll throw it in the garbage." Taking a quick look at it, she noticed that the top part of the paper was partially torn. But she recognized Warrenstone's crest. "Where did you get this from?" she asked Dexter.

"The bus stop near to Polly's Flower Shop."

"That's not too far from my house," she whispered. "Thanks. Okay class turn to page fifteen in your math workbook."

As her class continued, Detective Armstrong was standing next to forensic pathologist Mark Flores. He had an open file in his hand.

"Whoever was driving that car really hit him hard," Mark said.

"That person must have known that he or she had probably hit someone," the detective said. "And it must have happened not too far from Code's house."

"The person must have known they had hit him because Jasper Warren's foot had injuries to it that suggested it was in the air when it was hit."

"As if he was running. The person was chasing him. This isn't a hit and run, it's a run and hit."

The police identified a location to where the incident may have taken place, and it was cordoned off. Thanks to camera footage in the area, they got footage of Jasper sitting in the passenger seat of a car. There was not much to show the person who was driving it. Detective Armstrong couldn't make out if it was a male or female driving. He was stumped. No witnesses. And what he heard about the car later that day didn't bring the news he wanted.

He and fellow officers, along with Mark Flores, were standing next to a burnt out car. The car that they were looking for. The car they found out had been stolen.

Code was walking down the school's hallway as she headed for the exit. Her hand was on the door handle when Principal Turner called out her name.

"Not driving today?" Principal Turner asked.

"No, I got a ride with Maddie. How did you know I wasn't driving today?"

"I didn't see your car in the parking lot."

"Oh."

"Don't forget we have Big Brother and Big Sister Day tomorrow."

"It's one of the first things I mark down on my calendar every year."

"Okay, don't let me keep you."

"Goodbye, Principal Turner," she said.

"Janice, please. School's out. And goodbye, Code," she said, turning around and starting her usual walkabout through the school.

"Sorry," she said to Maddie, who was waiting in front of the school.

"I'm going to take you home so you can get some sleep," her best friend told her, starting the car.

"I'm not going home."

"What?" she asked, stopping the car.

"Don't stop the car," she said.

"Code, where are you going?"

"Polly's Flower Shop."

"But not to buy flowers."

"How do you know that?" she asked as Maddie started the car again.

"If I found a dead body in my yard, I'd be a total mess. You, not so much. Why are we going there?" Maddie asked.

"Because of this," Code said, opening her purse and taking out the paper Dexter had given her. "Since you're driving, I'll read it for you. 30 + 30 = 60 - 30 = 31."

"That's wrong, the answer should be 30," Maddie said.

"If Jasper dropped that piece of paper near the bus stop near the flower shop, he must have gotten injured nearby. Park in the parking lot and we'll start from—"

"We?"

"Oh best friend of mine."

"I'm going to—"

"We can start from the bus stop and go backwards," Code said.

"But that'll be taking you away from your house," Maddie said.

"Right."

"Ah, you want to see where he came from before he arrived at your house."

"Correct."

They walked backwards until they came to an alleyway. They were about to go down it when they heard sirens approaching.

"Code, what did you do?" Maddie asked.

"Nothing."

"Got any sleep, Miss Patterson?" a familiar voice asked.

"Detective Armstrong. Silas."

"Move them back, please," he told an officer as he himself went down the alley. "How far is forensic?" he asked out loud to the officer guarding the entrance of the alley.

"Five minutes away, sir."

"Thanks. The person took him to this alley and made him run down it only to knock him with the car. Thinking he was dead, that person left."

"Silas."

"Mark, I think we found our crime scene. CCTV showed the car entering this alley."

"I'll take a look," he said. "But before I do," he whispered, "about the phone call you made earlier. I looked up Terrence Miller's file."

"And?"

"And he was blind."

"I know. But how did a blind man murder a scientist?" he asked.

"Not only that, after leaving a business establishment, he tried crossing the street but was struck. He died at the scene."

"I don't think it's a coincidence that he also died ten years ago."

"I'll take a look at the crime scene," Mark said.

"Detective Armstrong!" Code called out as she waived a piece of paper in the air. He walked in her direction. And when he was close by she said, "I have something to show you."

"Step over this way, please," pointing with his head where he wanted them to go. "What is it?"

"This piece of paper that one of my students found at the bus stop near Polly's Flower Shop."

"Excuse me," he told her as he pulled out his phone and made a call.

"You're sending officers to the bus stop," she said, after he put his phone away.

"About that paper," he said, as she smiled. "You can stop smiling."

"Sorry. This partially torn paper has the Warrenstone College crest on it and a math equation that's wrong."

"What is it?" he asked.

"30 + 30 = 60 - 30 = 31."

"31. Wait right here." He walked over and, lifting the police caution tape, went out onto the sidewalk. He turned and walked left and then returned. He turned and walked right and then returned. He then walked over back to her. "Thanks," he said, as he began to walk away.

"What are you looking for?" she asked.

"Code, let's go," Maddie said, as she gently began pulling her friend away.

"Two minutes," she said. She went and did the same thing Detective Armstrong did. He noticed. "This alley was once a store, store 31."

After Maddie dropped her home, Code crashed on the sofa. And that was where she woke up hours later in darkness. It was now night and she felt really hungry. After something to eat and a shower, she took out her students' math workbooks and marked the work that they did.

With all school related things done, she turned her attention to the missing store, or the store that was there before the alley. Thanks to some research on the internet, she found out that it was a bookstore called Book Nut, and that it had closed down ten years ago. Other than those things, hardly anything interesting was mentioned. *I need to go to the library,* she said to herself.

"Is this the newspaper that has what I'm looking for?" Detective Armstrong asked the librarian as he held up the paper in question.

"Yes."

"Thanks," he said, walking off with the newspaper.

Finding a table, he put the paper on it and took a seat in a chair. No one else was around so he read it quietly to himself. *Terrence Miller, an employee of Book Nut, was struck and killed today as he left work. There were no witnesses and no CCTV footage of what happened. The owner, Tom Warren, was pretty shaken up when he heard about the incident. He told the police that he didn't know why Mr. Miller was at the store so late, seeing that it was closed.*

"The librarian told me that someone had the paper I was looking for."

"Miss Patterson," he said, without turning around.

"Edna, the librarian, said that the bookstore was closed because after the accident business went down," she said, taking a seat.

"Do sit down," he said.

"Thanks. The past owner, Mr. Tom Warren, is Jasper's father. Mr. Terrence Miller was the blind worker that was killed. He worked in the braille section of the store."

"Why do you need this paper?" he asked.

"His murder is unsolved. He has a son, James. I'm thinking–"

"Oh no."

"What if James blamed Mr. Warren for his dad's death and, ten years later, took it out on his son."

"I can't believe I'm going to tell you this," he said.

"Do tell," she said, getting out of her seat and going and sitting next to him.

"Mr. Warren had no idea what Mr. Miller was doing there. It was 11:15 p.m. The store had been closed since seven."

"We have to talk with Mr. Miller's wife." He cleared his throat. "You have to talk with Mr. Miller's wife."

"And with that," he said, standing up, "Goodnight, Miss Patterson."

"Will you ever call me Code?" she asked, also standing to her feet.

"We found some blood on the seat by the bus stop. It's being tested to see if it belongs to the victim."

"How about a cup of coffee?" she asked.

"How about you not make it a habit of not getting enough sleep."

"You're right. Goodnight, Silas," she said, leaving before him.

He watched her until she got in her car and drove away. *Why do I get the feeling that Jasper knew exactly where he was going when he got to your house?* he asked himself.

Bright and early the next morning, the diner brought over some treats for the day. Each year it contributed to the Big Brother and Big Sister Day. Some of the teachers had come in early to decorate. Code and Maddie were two of them. As usual, Principal Turner was the first one there. And she was making sure that everything was in order.

Some of the students lived at the Kids Home. Dexter was one of them. His Big Brother was in the army and was deployed, so he had to get a new one. They had been hanging out for the past four months. They liked each other and got along very well.

When Dexter showed up at school, Detective Armstrong was waiting for him. "Silas!" the nine-year-old called out, causing him to turn around.

"Good morning, Dexter. How are you?" he asked, wearing a big smile.

"Great."

"Cool."

"You're gonna have lots of fun today," he said. "There are games and a lot of nice things to eat."

"Perfect," he said, causing him to giggle. "Let's go in," he said, holding out his hand for the little boy to take it.

They went in and joined the others. Everyone had to sign in. After that, Detective Armstrong and Dexter headed to the auditorium. Code was standing in a corner when she saw them walk in.

"Oh, so cute," Maddie said. "No talking about bodies, please," she told Code as her best friend began to walk over to the detective.

"Good morning, Miss Patterson," Dexter said. "This is my Big Brother, Detective Silas Armstrong."

"Nice to meet you," she said, holding out her hand, which he took and shook.

"Miss Patterson is the reigning champion in the basketball shootout," Dexter said.

"Oh, is she now. Well," he said, doing some stretches, "I'll see if I can dethrone her."

Just then, Principal Turner walked on the stage and up to the microphone. She gave her opening speech and the event was officially started.

Lots of games. A whole lot of fun. Many photos were taken. Tasty treats in abundance. And all were sad to see it come to an end. But it did with a new reigning basketball shootout champion. It wasn't Detective Armstrong but Principal Turner, who had secretly been practicing with the help of her husband.

With all that over, and the school doors about to be locked, Maddie headed home after a very tiring day. Code went to the Warrens but didn't know what she was going to say. Detective Armstrong went to see Mark Flores, who was filled with questions about how the event at the school went.

"You'll make a great dad," he told Detective Armstrong.

"Mr. Miller isn't the suspect in Richard Patterson's murder, he was the witness."

"But he was blind."

"Maybe the killer didn't know that," the detective said. "But what if the killer knew, then–"

"If we solve the Miller Hit and Run, then we'll solve the Warren Run and Hit," Mark said.

"I think they're connected, but I don't believe it's the same killer."

"The blood at the bus stop belongs to Jasper."

"So he was driven to the alley," Detective Armstrong said.

"He's sitting in the passenger seat and he doesn't look scared," Mark said.

"Which meant he knew the person who took him to that alley and left him there thinking he was dead. He got up and managed to make it to the bus stop. But he didn't call for help."

"We didn't find a phone."

"And he went to Code's house. Why?"

"Does she know him?" asked Mark.

"No," Detective Armstrong said.

"Where is she now?" Mark asked.

"Oh no, the Millers' house," he said, rushing out.

But wrong house. Code was sitting in the living room of the Warrens. Mr. Warren wasn't home yet so she sat and talked with Mrs. Warren who had just returned from the kitchen. Putting a tray with a teapot and tea cups on the coffee table, she then took a seat.

"I'm so sorry about your son," Code told her.

"I don't understand who would want to do such a thing," Mrs. Warren said. "It must have been a shock to find him in your yard."

"Yes, it was. I'm sorry I didn't know him."

"He was nice and friendly," Mrs. Warren said, starting to cry.

Moving over to her, Code said, "It's going to be okay. I'm sure the police will catch whoever did this."

The front door of the house opened; Mr. Warren stepped in. When he saw Code, he immediately bent his head, as if not wanting her to see his face. She noticed.

Detective Armstrong had just pulled up to the Millers' residence. Exiting his car, he looked around to see if Code's car was nearby. He didn't see it or her. He walked up to the path to the house and rang the doorbell, hoping not to see her sitting on the sofa. He was pleased to find only Ms. Miller at home and that there were no other visitors.

"Such a question about what happened so long ago, but I remember it like it happened yesterday. No, Mr. Warren didn't call my husband that night. Terrence told me that it was a woman's voice."

"Maybe one of his co-workers," Detective Armstrong said.

"I don't know. Maybe."

"Did your husband ever work for Sandbook Corporation?"

"No, never heard of it. Are you asking these questions because there's a break in the case?"

"Maybe. But I don't want to get your hopes up," he said.

"I understand," she said.

"Where is your son, James?" he asked.

"He has a class. He was twelve when his father was murdered. He's been trying to solve it himself. He's still angry."

"Does he blame Mr. Warren?" Detective Armstrong asked.

"I'll be lying if I said no," she said.

"Is he angry enough to take it out on Jasper?" he asked, watching the nervousness of her hands.

She was about to answer when the front door opened. James stepped in. "I thought you had a class," she said, standing up and walking over to him to give him a hug.

"I didn't feel good so I decided to come home," he said, releasing the hug. Turning to the visitor, he asked, "Hello, Detective Armstrong, what are you doing here?"

"He's asking about your father," she said.

"You and Jasper were best friends, do–"

"I didn't kill him if that's where you're heading."

"I'm not heading anywhere. Do you remember anything else about that night?" he asked, standing to his feet.

"Jasper got a call that he didn't seem too happy about."

"Around what time?"

"Just before he left the diner around 9:33 p.m. After class, we went to the diner. Immediately after that call, he wrote something down on a piece of paper. I couldn't see what it was."

"Thanks," Detective Armstrong said. "I'll see myself out."

"What about my father?" James asked.

"If there's anything new, we'll let you know," he told them before he left. And just when he was walking to his car, Code was exiting hers.

"Looks like you beat me here," she told him.

"Why are you here?" he asked.

"I just stopped by to talk to Ms. Miller," she said.

"About?" She smiled. "Goodbye, Miss Patterson," he said, walking off.

"Code, please," she said loud enough so he could hear but the others in the house couldn't. Turning around, she felt a pang in her chest. She cried out loud, "Silas!" He came running back; Ms. Miller and her son came rushing out.

When she woke up, she was lying on a couch in the Millers' living room. James was in his room. His mom was sitting on the sofa. Detective Armstrong was sitting on the edge of the couch.

"Miss Patterson," he said, "are you okay?"

"What happened?" she asked.

"You fainted," he told her.

"Do you need to go to the hospital?" Ms. Miller asked.

"No, I'm fine. I just–"

"Was there something you wanted to ask me? Is that why you came?" she asked.

"I forgot," Code said.

"Must not have been important then," Ms. Miller said.

"I'm sorry."

"That's okay."

"I think I better take you home," Detective Armstrong said.

"What about my car?" she asked.

"I'll send an officer for it," he said, doing just that by making a call.

Offering her his hand, she took it and he helped her to his car. Ms. Miller stood by the door and watched them leave. No detours were taken, even though she asked to go somewhere. He drove her straight home.

"Thank you," she said, opening the car door.

"You didn't forget, did you?"

"Huh?"

"What was it that you wanted to ask her?" he asked.

She closed the car door. "On the night her husband was killed was he wearing a tan pants and a white T-shirt?"

"How do you know that?"

"Looks like I'm right. There are pieces to a puzzle in my head. But they're jumbled."

"Miss Patterson, I need you to think very carefully. Did you see Mr. Miller on the night he was killed?"

"Yes, but I can't remember where. It wasn't near the bookstore. I didn't know until recently that existed."

"Where did you see him?" he asked.

"I can't remember."

He was about to ask a question when his phone rang. He answered. After he was done, he put his phone away. "I have to go," he said.

"Why?" And there was that face with no smile again. "The officer brought my car," she said, getting out of his car.

He got out of the car, went to talk with the officer and then returned and got back into his car. He drove off. Out of curiosity she went to ask the officer what Detective Armstrong had told him.

"To wait for five minutes after he's gone to give you the keys to your car."

"Why?"

"So you won't follow him. And here are the keys, ma'am," he said, giving her the keys to her car. He then left in an awaiting squad car.

If these cases are connected, then the same person who killed Mr. Miller is the same person that killed Jasper, she said to herself. *I'm not sure.* She got into her car and drove to Maddie's house.

At the table in the interrogation room in the police station, Detective Armstrong sat on one side and James Miller sat on the other side. He was brought in for questioning when the owner of the diner told the police that she remembered him getting up and following Jasper outside around the time that he told the police that he had stayed in the diner.

"Why did you lie?" Detective Armstrong asked.

"Because I killed him."

"No, you didn't. Where did you go after you left the diner?"

"I followed him. He walked outside the diner for a few minutes before walking away from it. I followed him but he didn't go far."

"Where did he go?"

"He just stood there near to the diner, so I turned and went back inside. I got my bag and went home."

"What time was it?" Detective Armstrong asked.

"Twelve before ten. After I got my bag and headed out he was gone," James said.

"Is that the truth?" Detective Armstrong asked, standing to his feet.

"Yes," James said.

"Okay, you can go . . . for now," he told him as he opened the door and let him go.

Detective Armstrong wasted no time in heading over to collect and look at the belongings of the victim. But there was still no phone.

Code and Maddie were sitting at a table in Maddie's kitchen. They were eating slices of pizza that Code had ordered. She told her best friend what had happened.

"I'm surprised you still didn't follow him," Maddie said.

"He had a headstart and was nowhere in sight by then," Code said.

"But how do you know what clothes Mr. Miller wore if you never knew about it?" Maddie asked.

"I don't know."

"And why was Mr. Warren trying to hide his face?"

"I don't know that either. I remember going to my dad's lab and not finding him there," Code said.

"That was the night he was murdered, right?"

"Yes."

"I'm sorry for bringing it up," Maddie said.

"That's okay. I remember him having an argument earlier that day. Now that I think about it, it could have been Mr. Warren. I'm not sure," she said, shaking her head.

"Sorry. I couldn't have been more help."

"You having a listening ear is always a great help," she said, getting up and carrying her plate to the sink. "School night."

"Yes, early night," Maddie said, getting up and giving her friend a hug. "Goodbye. I love you."

"I love you too. But where exactly did I see Mr. Miller?" she asked.

"Maybe you should ask Detective Armstrong for help," she said, wearing a smile on her face.

"Why are you smiling?" Code asked.

"No reason."

"Later," she said, as she left.

Detective Armstrong had enlisted the help of Mark Flores and both of them were at Code's house where the body was found.

"What are we looking for again?" Mark asked, crawling on his knees in that area.

"Jasper's phone. We have to hurry up before Code comes home because–"

"Where is she?" he asked.

"Not here," the detective answered.

"Why not get the number from someone that knew him?"

"Because I might be alerting his killer," he said, reaching for something under a shrub. "Got it. Let's go."

"There is an old lady watching us from across the street," Mark said, as they both headed to the car.

"Wave and smile," he told him. They both did. And Ms. Harris waved and smiled back. They got in the car and drove off.

Hours later, Code was still not home yet, which concerned Maddie greatly. She tried calling her phone but it was turned off. She went to the only person she thought could help, Detective Armstrong. He was sitting at his desk in the station when she approached him.

"I don't know where else to go," she told him. Her voice was flustered.

"Please have a seat. What's the matter?" he asked.

"Code isn't home," she said.

"That's normal."

"No, she was at my house. When she left, she said that she was heading home."

"I'm sure she's okay," he told her.

"Her phone is off."

"Oh."

"She was also trying to figure out where she had seen Mr. Miller the night he was killed."

"Principal Turner is here to see you," an officer said, approaching his desk.

"Principal Turner," Maddie gasped. "Something must be seriously wrong."

He got up and went up front to see her; Maddie followed. "Is anything wrong, Principal Turner?" he asked.

"Oh no, I just came to drop off your certificate for participating in the Big Brother, Big Sister Day. But it looks like I should ask Maddie if anything is wrong."

"We're just having a conversation," Maddie said.

"I saw Code about two hours ago, but I don't think she saw me. She was with Mr. Warren."

"Jasper's dad?" Maddie asked.

"Yes."

"I'm relieved," Maddie said, as a slight smile came across her face. Detective Armstrong wasn't relieved, and didn't show it. "I think I'll head home now," she said.

"I'll walk out with you," Principal Turner said, giving the certificate to Detective Armstrong before walking off with Maddie.

After they were gone, he put out an APB on Mr. Warren. He knew that he wasn't going to use his own car. He had a car dealership where a lot of cars were available to him.

Pulling out Richard Patterson's case file, he took out a paper out of it and read it. Rushing out of the station, he went to his car. He told two officers to go to the Millers' residence and carry them to the location he specified. He also said to bring Mrs. Warren.

He was in that location sitting in darkness . . . waiting. Twenty-five minutes after eleven, a car stopped at the entrance of the alley. A man stepped out and, going over to the passenger side, forcibly removed a woman from the car. From where he was sitting, he knew it was Code. The man he suspected was Mr. Warren, who untied Code's hands and pulled the tape from off her mouth.

"You killed your son," she said.

"He was going to reveal a secret that he shouldn't," he said.

"And what would that be?" she asked, trying to escape.

"Don't think about it," he said.

"Think about what?" Detective Armstrong asked. He had silently exited his car and walked up behind them.

"He killed his son," Code said, "but I don't think he killed Mr. Miller."

"Because he didn't." Taking out his phone, he made a call and two squad cars appeared. One was carrying the Millers; the other was carrying Mrs. Warren. They all exited and made their way towards him. "Now that we're all here."

"What's going on?" Code asked.

"Jasper died before he had a chance to tell you," Detective Armstrong said, turning to her.

"Who killed my son?" Mrs. Warren asked. "Was it James?"

"My son didn't kill anyone," Ms. Miller said, jumping to her son's defence.

"Why is this alley so important?" the detective asked. "Because it was a store ten years ago. It was because of this store that Mr. Miller was lured out of his house way after it was closed."

"I didn't kill him," Mr. Warren said.

"No, but your wife did," he said, causing all eyes to turn in her direction.

She began to say, "I didn't–"

"I first thought that the killer probably didn't know that he was blind, but then the planted fake name tag at the murder scene proved to me that she knew."

"What crime scene?" they all asked in unison.

"I was trying to protect you," she said to her husband.

"You killed my dad," James said, moving in her direction, causing the detective to signal to one of the officers to hold him back.

"Miss Patterson heard an argument between a man and her father. What you didn't know was that she was unsure it was actually you. Later that day, she went over to her father's lab but he wasn't there."

"That's right," Code said. "Was that because Mr. Warren had him?"

"I'm sure when we take your fingerprints they'll match the only one that was left at the crime scene that hadn't been identified."

"You killed my father?" Code asked. "But why?"

"It was an accident," Mr. Warren said. "The reason we argued was because he had refused to have his book signing at my bookstore. I'm sure that would have boosted traffic. He went with my rival."

"But why kill him?" she asked.

"I was still very angry after our argument. I went to his office and forced him to go with me."

"But unknown to you, Mr. Warren, was that your wife also went there."

"She did?" he asked. "Why?"

"I was going to try to persuade him to also do a book signing at the store. But I saw you forcing him into your car. I followed you. Only you came out of that warehouse," she said, beginning to cry. "I waited to see if Mr. Patterson was going to come out. But he never did."

"So you went into protection mode," Detective Armstrong said. "You put a fake name tag near the body."

"Yes. It was a prop that I had made for a play. Terrence's name was on it because it was a sample that he had helped me make," Mrs. Warren said.

"You called Mr. Miller, causing him to leave his house. And you waited near the bookstore."

"Yes," she said.

"That's how I knew what he was wearing," Code said. "I had seen him."

"Yes, but before he had reached the bookstore," Detective Armstrong said. "When Mr. Miller saw that the store was closed, the street that he had crossed countless times safely became unsafe. There were no other cars around. He stepped off that sidewalk–"

"Stop!" shouted Ms. Miller, beginning to cry.

"Your son found out. Don't know how."

"One night he overheard my wife and I talking about Mr. Patterson's murder," Mr. Warren said. "We thought he was asleep."

"I didn't know he knew," Mrs. Warren said. "You killed our son. I would have rather gone to prison than you take his life."

"Mr. Tom Warren, I'm arresting you for the murders of Mr. Richard Patterson and Jasper Warren. Mrs. Maria Warren, I'm arresting you for the murder of Mr. Terrence Miller. Officers, read them their rights and take them away."

They were read their rights while being taken to separate squad cars.

"Thank you," James said to Detective Armstrong before he and his mom left.

When he was alone with her he asked, "Miss Patterson, are you okay?"

"Code, please," she said, bursting out in tears.

Drawing her closer to him and hugging her, he said, "Code."

From Vilia Amertil other books

Polly Parish Mysteries Book 1 - With the reluctant help of her five adopted brothers, thirteen-year-old Polly Parish attracts danger in her quest in solving crimes and bringing criminals to justice.

Pastor Thomas is Missing: Maybe 1 Timothy 6 vs 10

Taking out her What Happened Today book, she read what she had written down the night before. And she knew exactly where that piece of cloth came from. *But why would the church's secretary want to climb through the pastor's office?* she thought. Polly knew that she needed to find out. But how was she going to do that if she couldn't leave the house? Unless . . .

"We're gonna be in big trouble if Mom and Dad find out about this," Silas said, as he helped his brothers and sister slowly and carefully push Jacob's car down their driveway.

"Whose bright idea was this again?" asked Joshua.

"Polly's," all her brothers said in unison.

"I want to know," began Caleb, "how are all of us going to fit in this car?"

"We're going to tie you to the roof," Paul said.

"But I'll fall off," Caleb said, taking Paul, who was only joking, seriously.

"Not if we tie you tight," Paul said.

"Okay, this is far enough. Let's all get in," Jacob said.

"Does everyone have a flashlight?" Polly asked. As if that was his cue, Caleb turned on his flashlight and accidentally shined it in Polly's face. "Thanks for trying to blind me," she told him.

"Sorry," he said.

"No problem," she told him.

"Listen up everyone, it's now 1:09 a.m. We're gonna go by the church and look for what again," Jacob said, turning to Polly.

"Anything that shouldn't be there," she said.

"Ah, great," said Paul, "that can be anything."

"Let me finish. I wish we were doing this during the day."

"Now she tells us," Jacob said, rolling his eyes and pulling up to the church at the same time.

"Look for a broken heel or torn pieces of cloth in the area of the pastor's office," she said.

"That'll be like looking for a needle in a haystack," Silas said.

"I'll go look for it," said Polly, as she got out of the car, "and you guys can stay here."

"Why should we care anyway that Ms. Sapphira Wilson, the church's secretary, climbed through the pastor's office?" asked Joshua.

"One million dollars," she said, walking away. That caused all of them to exit the car and join her. "If you find anything interesting, put them in your bags and we'll sort them out when we get home."

They missed their cut off time by one minute when they arrived home. It was now 1:46 a.m. and not the 1:45 a.m. that they were aiming for. Each carried their bags and the things they found to their rooms. A bright light morning would be better to sort them out. And the fact that all of them were very sleepy helped in that decision.

Before breakfast, they all headed to the TREE HUT, including Polly. Emptying their bags, a whole bunch of things fell out. A pencil. A pack of chewing gum. An old raggedy tennis ball. Just to name a few. No broken heel or torn pieces of cloth.

"Well that was a bust," Paul said, as he and his brothers turned to leave.

"Wait," said Polly. "Everyone is thinking that Pastor Thomas ran off with that check, but what if he didn't?"

"Nothing that we just poured out of our bags proves that he didn't do it," Jacob said.

"But what about this?" Polly asked as she poured out the last item out of her bag.

They were all speechless as they stood there. They were looking down at Pastor Thomas' bloody shirt. The same one he wore on Sunday.

Feed Me Fatal, If Only James 1 vs 19

"You're saying," Mr. Parish began, "that Abel Miller was the only one that was eating out of a white bowl last evening."

"Yes," said Polly. "Everyone else had black bowls. We need to get back into that kitchen."

"Why?" asked Mr. Parish.

"Whoever it was that locked me in the freezer probably was hiding the bowl in the kitchen."

Jacob said, "The only person I noticed in the kitchen was Rupert Cain. But I'm not saying that he's the one that locked you in the freezer."

"Interesting," said Polly. "Dad, may we go there before school starts?"

"How about I call the police and they, and not you or anyone else sitting around this table, can go down there."

"Polly and Silas don't be late for your bus," Mrs. Parish told them.

They went to the same school. Polly was in grade nine; Silas was in grade eight. Their other siblings went to another school. They didn't take the bus. Jacob drove all of them there.

Standing at the bus stop waiting for their bus, Polly asked, "Silas, you like solving things, don't you?"

"Not if they get me in trouble and–"

"This won't get us in trouble."

"Whatever it is, I don't think so."

"Let me cut to the chase," she said.

"Are we going to chase someone?" he asked.

"Never mind."

The school bus came; she missed the opportunity to go to the kitchen in the hall to search for that bowl. It wasn't until lunchtime, when they were allowed to leave the school's campus for lunch, that Polly went in search of that bowl.

She didn't have a lot of time. The hall was opened and she went into the kitchen. No one was in there when she began her search. The bowl was out in the open. *Maybe the person didn't have enough time to hide it,* she thought. *But maybe they did hide it in plain sight.*

Going into her detective bag, she pulled out a large plastic bag big enough to fit that bowl. She carefully put it in and then put that bag into her detective bag. All this was done with gloves on.

She was just about to leave when she heard someone coming. She quickly tried to hide when the kitchen door was pushed open.

"Stop!" the person yelled.

Unwanted Christmas Present, But Not Luke 2 vs 14

Paul looked at his sister and asked, "What are you up to?"

"Nothing," she said.

"R-i-i-ight," said Jacob.

"Yeah, right," Paul said, following his brother downstairs.

"You guys are always suspicious," she said, following her brothers.

Paul entered the kitchen and searched through the pantry once again. He found an unopened bottle of teriyaki sauce and didn't have to go to the store anymore.

While he and Caleb were in the kitchen trying to make dinner, the rest of the family, except Mrs. Parish, were outside. She was sitting at the bay window as she looked out at the snowball fight. That's when a car came driving up the driveway. Polly knew that car. It belonged to Mr. Shepherd.

"You can always have fun in a snowball fight," he said, exiting his car.

"Mr. Shepherd, what brought you here?" Mr. Parish asked.

"Brought some new smoke detectors for you. The fire station usually gives some out at Christmas."

"Thanks," said Mr. Parish.

Jacob, Joshua, and Silas continued with the snowball fight as Polly went over to Mr. Shepherd's car. He and her father were having a conversation. Mrs. Parish went upstairs to use the bathroom.

Nothing of interest piqued Polly's interest until she went over to the passenger side of the car. There it was, the red gas can with the orange stripe. The one that she had seen Teddy Wiseman carrying.

Mrs. Parish came out of the bathroom and went over by the window in her bedroom. Looking out, she saw her children having a snowball fight and her husband conversing with someone. She was about to step away when she saw her daughter getting into the backseat of the visitor's car.

By that time, the conversation between her husband and Mr. Shepherd was over and he was getting into his car. Starting it, he drove off, unaware that Polly was crouched down in the backseat.

Mrs. Parish stood at the window as she watched in horror. She turned around and rushed downstairs.

The Night Cats by Jessica Amertil Ling and Vilia Amertil

When a valuable pin goes missing, twelve-year-old Eiffel Jeunesse from France, along with her shy neighbor, Sam Grey, team up to find it, bringing danger and adventure their way.

Sam ran after her, wishing Eiffel wouldn't run so fast. When he got to her, Eiffel was sitting down on a rock and writing something on the ground in French. When she saw him, she stood up and pointed up ahead.

"There's a diviser in the path."

"What does a diviser mean?" he asked.

"In anglaise? Don't know."

Sam sighed. He asked, "Which way should we go now?"

"Right," Eiffel said shakily.

"What?" Sam cried. "Did you see Mr. Jones go that way?"

"No. But trust me. We need to go right," she said more surely this time.

"But if you get us lost . . ."

Sam couldn't finish that sentence because he didn't want to think about what would happen to them.

"I won't," she said, smiling. That made Sam a little more confident than he thought. "Let's go."

They treaded lightly because the ground was covered with dead leaves that made echoing sounds every time they stepped on them. Sam, for his part, kept on looking back, as if he thought someone was following them. But no one was. He was just extremely nervous. That nervousness of looking back caused him to bump into Eiffel, who had stopped.

"Sam," she whispered.

"Sorry," he whispered back. "Why are we stopping?"

"Mr. Jones is just standing there," she said.

"Do you think he heard us?" he asked.

Mr. Jones walked over to a tree and took out some papers that were in it. A short strong wind blew in and one of the papers slipped out of his hands. He was moving to go after it but stopped.

The paper that had flown away landed next to Eiffel, who slowly and quietly picked it up.

"It looks like a buyer for the pin," she whispered.

"I want to know if he saw us," Sam whispered.

She was about to answer when Mr. Jones quickly turned in their direction. He couldn't see them, though. They were greatly hidden behind a big tree.

"Who's there?" Mr. Jones asked.

Don't miss out!

Visit the website below and you can sign up to receive emails whenever Vilia Amertil publishes a new book. There's no charge and no obligation.

https://books2read.com/r/B-A-WEJT-ZTDAC

BOOKS2READ

Connecting independent readers to independent writers.

About the Author

From the Caribbean, Vilia Amertil says, "Hello."
Read more at https://whatisgoingoninyourworld.wordpress.com/.